THIS WALKER BOOK BELONGS TO:

_____

_____

_____

sleeping

dancing

crying

waving

giving

eating

skipping

telling

listening

thinking

yawning

kicking

smelling

stroking

giving

shouting

washing

writing

singing

tearing

For Mark

First published 1993 by Walker Books Ltd
87 Vauxhall Walk, London SE11 5HJ

This edition published 2005

2 4 6 8 10 9 7 5 3 1

© 1993 Shirley Hughes

The right of Shirley Hughes to be identified as
author/illustrator of this work has been asserted by her in
accordance with the Copyright, Designs and Patents Act 1988

This book has been typeset in Plantin

Printed in China

British Library Cataloguing in Publication Data:
a catalogue record for this book is available from the British Library

ISBN 1-84428-530-8

www.walkerbooks.co.uk

Giving

Shirley Hughes

WALKER BOOKS
AND SUBSIDIARIES

LONDON • BOSTON • SYDNEY • AUCKLAND

I gave Mum a present on her birthday,
all wrapped up in pretty paper.

And she gave me a big kiss.

I gave Dad a very special picture
which I painted at play-group.

And he gave me a ride on his
shoulders most of the way home.

I gave Olly some slices
of my apple.

We ate them sitting under the table.

At teatime Olly gave me
two of his soggy crusts.

That wasn't much of a present!

You can give
someone a
cross look...

or a big smile!

You can give a tea party…

or a seat on a crowded bus.

On my birthday Grandma and Grandpa
gave me a beautiful doll's pram.
I said "Thank you" and gave
them each a big hug.

And I gave my dear Bemily
a ride in it, all the way down the
garden path and back again.

I tried to give the
cat a ride too,

but she gave me a
nasty scratch!

So Dad had to give my poor arm a kiss and
a wash and a piece of sticking plaster.

Sometimes, just when
I've built a big castle
out of bricks,

Olly comes along and
gives it a big swipe!
And it all falls down.

Then I feel like
giving Olly a big
swipe too.

But I don't, because

he *is* my baby brother, after all.

sleeping

dancing

crying

waving

giving

eating

skipping

telling

listening

thinking

yawning

kicking

smelling

stroking

giving

shouting

washing

writing

singing

tearing

WALKER BOOKS is the world's leading
independent publisher of children's books.
Working with the best authors and illustrators
we create books for all ages, from babies
to teenagers – books your child will
grow up with and always remember. So…

FOR THE BEST CHILDREN'S BOOKS,
LOOK FOR THE BEAR